A Kingdom Subsides

PARABLES OF THE KINGDOM OF GOD

By John S. Hodgkins

DEDICATION

Dedicated to my wife Tami, who has been with me
through all of this, my son Zachary and my daughter Bella,
whom I love dearly.

To David and Jim, who have walked
with God with me.

CONTENTS

1. Hinges – "Doing Their Work"

2. Parables – "The Love of God"

3. Electricity – "Current"

4. Coffee – "Stagnant"

5. Hush – "Peace Be Still"

6. Candle – "Into the Darkness"

7. Plant – "Call Me Deeper"

8. Abandoned – "Love"

9. Wall – "Capturing the Light"

10. What is God Stirring?

11. Cell Phone – "Resonate"

12. Among Them – "Humility"

13. Pie – "From the Inside"

14. Impenetrable – "Armor"

15. Coal – "Light on the Outside"

16. Adapting – "To the Will of God"

17. Rice – "Saturate our Soul"

18. Jack the Giant – "Humility"

19. Barbeque – "Peace"

20. Catapult Toy – "Perception"

21. The Time Machine – "Control"

22. Behavior – "Walking in the Spirit"

23. Mike & Linda – "Relationship with God"

24. The Prayers Below the Surface – "Dirt"

"I can do all this through him who gives me strength"
Philippians 4:13

INTRODUCTION

Have you ever wondered what it would be like to walk in the Kingdom of God ... hear His voice ... do His will ... have your life be completely submissive to Him? Mess up sometimes—sure—but walk in His mercy and grace? A dad, walking with you all the time.

To walk with the peacemaker. He heals your soul. He fathers you. He walks with you. Showing you His purposes and watching out for your own. You are not His Kingdom owner; you are His son or daughter. A child of the King. Much more than a servant. Waiting for His voice.

It's like walking with your father as Jesus did.

I've been reading John Eldredge books for years, and he talks about walking with God. There was a time in my journey where I needed to hear Jesus' voice. It was something new to me at the time, but now it is quite familiar.

He is that still, small voice in the quiet of the morning that calms and comforts me. Gives me peace. Sends me "forth" to do His will. "His Kingdom come."

On this journey, I asked God what He thought of me. Many words came to mind, but the most poignant for me was when He called me "my son." You are too, by the way. What He said to me was confusing at the time. I thought, Why is He calling me "son?" Jesus is His Son, so how can I be His son? That doesn't make any sense.

But it occurred to me that we are children of God. I had never thought of it that personally. You are too. We are children of God if we've accepted Jesus Christ as our Savior.

But why did He call me "son?" It was so … personal. Believing was not what I expected. But then He said, "I am your Father," and it blew me away. Why would He tell me that He is my Father? I needed to hear it. We all need to hear it. God not only loves us, but He wants to walk with us through the day, for His Spirit to move in us.

I had never experienced this. But I looked it up in Scripture and started to notice where God walked with His people. They were not alone. It was not up to them. He is with us. Centered in Christ is the way to live—not on our own.

We are here to walk with Him, to rest in His presence, to be with Him, to abide in Him. We are to walk close to His heart, as He walks with us, close to ours.

1. HINGES – " DOING THEIR WORK "

I have hinges on the back of my office door. I come in and put my coat on the hanger. I sit in front of my computer. I drink my cup of coffee, and I do my work. I have no recollection of the hinges, although I have been in this same office for about two years.

And yet, there they hang. They are doing their work. I don't notice them from day to day, but they are there. And they don't wonder if I ever notice them. They do their work faithfully.

I go home to sleep, after leaving the office, and they are still there.

I come in early in the morning, or late at night, and they are still there. They are doing the work they were faithfully called to do so many years ago.

As a matter of fact, they never left. Whether I see them or not, whether I notice them or not, they are faithfully doing their work.

No one has seen them for years. But now I do … and they are faithful.

I also think of the other things in my office. The picture on the wall, which has a nail holding it up. The nail is never seen. Or there is the t-shirt underneath the winter coat, or the sticks behind the woven decoration, and the padding beneath a helmet, or the studs behind the wall.

They are all faithfully doing their work, and they are never seen.

Only when they were put together, and maybe years down the road if they are ever taken apart, would they be seen again.

I think about the electricity behind the wall and the pages with words inside a beautifully bound book. I think of the seeds in the packet on my bookshelf. They are bursting to get out and do their work.

I think of the inside of a cup, which is rarely noticed. Or the inside of my thermos, which keeps things cold and hot.

I also notice the nails in a little wooden crate, and the rocks beneath a photo of Niagara Falls that make the falls jut out. But still, they remain unseen.

I think of all these things.

They remain unseen but do their work. Day. After. Day.

2. PARABLES – " THE LOVE OF GOD "

I love parables. I love stories and allegories and movies and anything that can tell a point without giving it all away, to show us our true heart's desire. Not in a way of dutifully pushing us in a direction our heart does not want to go.

I love to watch movies, like the DC comics television show "Arrow," which tells of an arrogant, rich playboy who cares about nobody but himself. But is broken to the core through a difficult five-year excursion and becomes the man he was meant to be.

I also love stories like the 2005 television series "Prison Break," where a man gets himself into prison to help his brother who was wrongly accused.

Now that is a redemption story.

No matter what kind of story—how redemptive or hideous—there is always some sort of allegory in it. Something where we can get a glimmer of what is really going on in the world in a way we can understand.

That is why Jesus told parables. So, in a simple way, we could be told what to do—but in the seat of our hearts. Not trying to earn favor with God, but being blessed by all the goodness of God in a simple message. Of course it must line up with the principles of God's word for us to be able to apply it to our lives as Christians. But starting with His principles, these stories can make us aware of greater things in the Kingdom of God.

My hope is that as you read these stories, you will find a pathway into your own journey … your deeper walk with God.

3. ELECTRICITY – " CURRENT "

The light was shut off. The switch was scratched on the plate, and it was not working anymore. It had once.

The switch plate was scratched and worn where many hands had touched it over the years. But now they were all silent.

Until the hands reached out to the electricity again, it would not do its work for them.

They were stagnant. They were waiting; yet now, they waited in the dark.

The light had not worked for years, because they had not applied their sciences—their theories of how the light works.

It was promised. The light. They thought about switching on the light, but their thoughts were not enough. Without engaging it, they had no light. It had been working in the past but not now.

4. COFFEE – " STAGNANT "

The coffee poured out of the pot almost scalding hot. We waited for it to boil. It boiled in place, waiting for the right time to come out and sit in the cup and steam.

It was a red mug with white scratches inside from the spoon going 'round and 'round over the years … stirring in the sugar and mix-ins: caramel, chocolate and lavender. Even tea occasionally. Well, I had tried tea once, but it didn't strike my fancy.

Coffee was the way to go for this stirrer of the morning. And pedestals. The mugs were placed on pedestals, so they could attain to this higher purpose of mixing these cups.

They stood still as they were stirred from above.

'Round and 'round they went. Stirred in circles. Not coming out.

5. HUSH – " PEACE BE STILL "

The child was sleeping in the darkness. His mother was at the other end of the house and couldn't see him in the darkness. He waited, and he didn't see his mother, so he started to cry. And he cried and cried and cried until finally his mother opened the door.

The door creaked as she opened it, and she peeked in. Light came into the room, and then she crept in and walked over to the child as light fell upon his crib. He started to cry.

His mother lifted the child into her arms and held him and started to rock her baby back and forth, back and forth. Then she put him down again in the crib, and the child started to cry. She lifted him up again; he returned to her arms, and she held him and started to walk around the room.

She walked over to the window and lifted up the shades, and they looked up together at the full moon lighting up the outside of the house and onto the windowsill. She shut the shades again and entered the darkness of the room and put down the child who was comforted now, and had started to sleep.

6. CANDLE – " INTO THE DARKNESS "

I looked out, over the hills, into the darkness and saw darkness.

We shouted to all the people in the darkness, but they could not hear us. It was muffled from inside the walls of our light place.

There was a fire burning where we were, and we wanted others to come and see it and get out of the cold. But all they could hear was hollow roars, so we went to them.

First it was a little boy with a stick.

He was playing with it from the fire.

He was almost burned as he picked up one stick but he—more than the rest of us—knew the importance. So he went outside with his stick. When the light was in his eyes, in the darkness he couldn't see very much. Only himself. And he knew what he wanted—to be in the light. And not to drop it, but he also wanted to rescue the others who were out there … to bring them out of the cold.

Someone came out next to him and before he knew, they had thrown their stick at a passerby. It missed, and it went out. Then another man came and tried to hand the hot end to another passerby, but it was too hot to handle so he dropped it and ran away.

They thought that the man was there to hurt them, but he wasn't; he was just trying to help. They didn't seem to understand.

The little boy gently walked over to a man who was trying to make a meal with no light. He let him use his stick to build a fire, so he could make his meal. The man was thankful.

But when the little boy went back home, he left the stick with the man. The man was grateful. The man then shared with another neighbor what the little boy had done and how they could make their meals much better with a little bit of light.

They were delighted.

7. PLANT – " CALL ME DEEPER "

My roots were deep and buried. No one could call to me. I was on my own.

I wanted my way. I was stuck. I didn't want any other way.

But there was another calling … a call from above.

Calling me out of myself to another, to another way of growing and learning.

Surrender.

Called out of where I had been, this dark place, up into the light.

I was following, and I would find the way as I was being drawn near.

I was growing from the inside out and waiting for my time, for my solitude.

But now the time had come.

I was ready. Groaning.

I was sounding out. Ready for my call.

I wanted to come out of the ground.

Out of this deadness, and I was ready.

I came out into the light.

And I was solid and full and light.

8. ABANDONED – " LOVE "

Derik was abandoned at birth and by the time he was 19 years old, he was a mess. He had been through drug and alcohol rehabs from the time he was 14. When he was out on the streets, he joined any gang or group of kids that he thought would take him in. Clinging to anybody and everybody.

His life was a mess.

The only skills he had were how to hurt people and how to keep them at a distance. He didn't know anything else. He wanted to deep down, but he didn't even know where to begin.

Why would his mother do this to him? Why would she abandon him at birth? He must have been worthless for this to happen. He didn't matter. He didn't care. He was nothing.

But one day he saw a voice. I don't mean the actual words, but a voice in action.

He had heard many voices before threatening him, mocking him on the playground, egging him on to get in one more punch.

But he was nothing, and he knew it. His mother's voice was different. He knew it. It would have been kind and helpful and sweet and nurturing. But not these voices. They were hateful and hurtful and well … not his.

Then he heard this voice.

The woman that it came out of was old and weak. She was frail from the inside out; she didn't have much to offer him—a tough street kid—but she was there and she was kind or so the voice made him believe.

She said his name, "Derik."

It pierced him and scared him all at once.

It jogged him from the inside out and crept all over him. No one should know his name. Especially not her, a perfect stranger. She crept inside him and made him want to fall apart. It was unnerving.

She should not know him, but she did.

Why? Where did she come from? How could she know him? Who was she?

So he worked up the courage, "What?"

"I have something for you," she said with tender eyes.

Who was this woman, and how would she know me? Why would she give anything to me?

The tenderness of her eyes made him give in … for he had been longing for kindness all his life.

It was a flower.

He had reached out his hand ever so gently toward the old woman, and she had placed a flower in his hand. Again he was wondering. Trying to put it all together.

"What is this for?" he asked.

"It's from your Mother," she said. And those words set him off. "Noooooooooooo!!!!!"

"Get out of here you witch, you demon. Show yourself to someone else but not to me."

But she was silent.

Her kindness wore away at his soul.

He spoke again. "What is this for? You know my mother's dead. That's what I've been told my whole life."

"But she's not," the old woman said with a commanding presence.

He listened.

"I have known her your whole life," she responded. "She has been in prison across the country and had to let you go. She wasn't allowed to keep you, so she would rather have you abandoned to a better way."

"It wasn't a better way," he replied. "It was wrong. It was selfish. You have no idea what's she's done to me."

"Yes, I do," said the woman. "I was there. At your birth. I was there through the ages."

9. WALL – " CAPTURING THE LIGHT "

There is a light in our kitchen. Not bright enough in the early morning to reach the outer walls.

When I get up and go around the corner toward the outside door, there is a wall where the light does not reach. No matter how bright and poignant the kitchen light is, it cannot penetrate this wall on its own.

So it waits.

Until sunrise. And then?

Out of the darkness, outside these walls comes a much greater light.

It can reach these unreachable walls.

The light shines brightly from the outside and shines in, to these dark places. And they can see again.

10. WHAT IS GOD STIRRING?

What is God stirring? I would encourage you to stop for a minute and ask God what He is stirring in your soul. Is there any message He wants you to hear? Is there anything in your mind? What is God stirring. What does He want you to hear?

Quiet now.

11. CELL PHONE – " RESONATE "

My cell phone was buzzing on the surface of my desk.

It reverberated to larger decibels as its sound waves resonated. The slight hum turned into a louder, magnified sound that could be heard around the office walls.

I could resonate with that sound. I had heard it before. When it was on my pillow, earlier that morning, I could barely hear it. But on this surface, the speech became louder.

It's like God talking.

In my soul, I can resonate with the voice of God in me. You can too, if you are living in the right plane.

We should be in touch. In tune. With what we are hearing and then those around us will start to feel its effect as well.

A cell phone sitting there—limp—doesn't do anybody much good. It's not getting those electronic impulses through the air, or at least not acting upon them.

"Pick it up," shouts the reverberating sound. "Act."

And you will—if you are paying attention.

12. AMONG THEM – " MY HUMILITY "

The eagle perched on the ledge high above the land. He could see all of creation. He wanted to see more. He wanted to see the lows and the highs … the people and the plains as they stretched out over the land.

He saw the people below and wanted to be closer. He wanted to be with them. Abide with them.

But he was not enough. He was the master of all creation—up above—but he wanted to be with them down below.

He went down below with eagle's wings. He soared down to them to see what he could see.

He wanted to be with them … but wait.

As he got closer, he could see the meanness of their souls. He would see them doing things to each other, unheard of up above. But he wanted to be with them anyway. He wanted to touch their souls with the great up above, to soar with them, to be with them.

But then he noticed they didn't have wings.

How could they fly if they didn't have wings?

And it would take a light spirit to make them soar.

Then he had an idea.

He would give them his wings, then they would be able to fly above to the sky, to the stars.

But then he thought, No.

All he had was one pair of wings, and he wanted to give it to them all.

So he started with one, and there the receiver went up into the sky.

No gratitude, just wings, soaring up into the sky.

He knew what he must do. He talked to them one at a time—all the people. He wanted to lift them up one at a time. So he asked them if they wanted to go up high with him. And they did. So he lifted them up one at a time. Without wings. And they flew.

13. PIE – " FROM THE INSIDE "

I turned toward a round pie, and I saw a brown crust. I looked at another, and it was the same. Brown in and brown out. All I could see was brown. Golden on top. But I wasn't sure what was on the inside.

Some had crisscrosses, and others had layers. Others still had lattices or wavy edges, but for most of them I could not tell what was on the inside from the outside.

Who can tell?

The baker. The one who made them all; he or she could tell. He could be wise to the matter. He could see the delight of each of the tender nuances, the sweetness, the tanginess, the zestiness. The baker can see them all from the inside out.

14. IMPENETRABLE – " ARMOR "

Stew didn't want to leave his cabin.

He woke up at about 3:00 a.m. The coals of his fire had a slight glow. He was warm and cozy inside, but he heard a noise on the outside. A soft pelting at first, and then it got louder.

His wife and kids were sleeping. He wanted to go outside, but he was scared. He had fallen asleep on the floor near the fireplace and woke up alone. His wife and kids were snuggled safely in their beds.

He approached the door and then heard another pelting. Little by little he heard stones against a window, but then it stopped.

He was about to go back to bed, but there it was again.

He approached the doorknob and reached out to touch the cold steel.

It was warm from the outside. He felt the anger of his enemy approaching, and he didn't know how he could have gotten so close to the house without him noticing. They had been far away the last he knew, but they were approaching. They were on foot, but they must have been moving all night.

He stole his way out to the shed—hiding behind tree after tree, considering the distant darkness. No enemy in sight, but he knew they were there. He could sense them at his feet.

He made his way to the shed and unlocked the rusty door.

He was opening a door to his past from inside the corner of the shed. The shed held a large trunk with weapons he had once used long ago. He started to open the trunk, and the pelting began against the shed. He knew they were out there waiting for him.

He stopped for a moment.

In the quiet of his mind, he recalled his trainer and all the training he had lost in his mind from years ago.

The recent years had been more pleasant. He had enjoyed his wife and child and more recently their newborn.

But now they were here again, and he would have to fight. The enemy had come to his door.

His great, great grandfather had been a knight in the English war long ago. He had a steed and a lance and now, before his eyes, was his ancient grandfather's armor.

Next to the armor was a canister of bludé. It was dark as pitch. He lathered it over his ears and into his hair. He worked it down his arms and over his legs. It completely covered his body. When he was covered in the bludé, he was almost unstoppable. He could hide anywhere in the darkness and could not be seen.

He could sneak into the enemy camp and take them out without them even touching him. He had to remember the bludé before he could put on the rest of the armor.

First he put on the belt, to which everything else was attached. Then he put on his breastplate and covered his iron boots he had prepared for just this occasion. Then he put on the helmet. It would protect his head from any evil that came his way. He slid the sword into the sheath on the side of his belt. It was as sharp now as ever. As a matter of fact, it never seemed to dull. It was useless when he had it in his case. It was a mighty weapon in his hand. One the enemy just couldn't refute.

Finally his shield. It had a molded leather strap on the back that he could grip tightly. When he held it upright, it covered from the top of his head down below his knees and was made of steel. He had a mark of his army on it, a cross to remind him who he stood for.

He walked toward the enemy camp under the cover of darkness. Sneaking from tree to tree, keeping his eyes far ahead into the distant darkness. As he got closer, he could see the speck of light that was their fireplace. It grew as he got closer, and he could smell smoke. And he could see the fire dancing in the wind.

He could hear the rumbling of the men around the fire. They were large with dark armor ready to sneak through the night as he had done.

He stepped on a twig behind a tree, and they all looked. They knew he was there, but he kept silent. Eventually they turned away as a few of them walked closer but lost interest as he wasn't doing anything special.

He walked around the enemy camp and through the forest on the other side. Even though it was the middle of the night, he came to a bright clearing. The light shone like the day. He saw a woman laying in the middle of the field hurt and bandaged. He started to walk over to her to help. She looked at him in tears and as he was about to speak, there was a ping on the back side of his armor. Someone had hit him with something.

As he was turning, a few more pings. It was like someone was pelting him with tiny stones that were soon growing larger. He looked back at the woman and then in the direction of the pelting. Fear came over him and as it grew in him, he shifted the weight of his shield toward the pelting and the fear went away. He knew he had blocked it out for now.

He knelt beside the woman and helped mend her bandage. He put on a fresh dressing and bandaged it up. As he stood, the pelting began again. But he got the woman to her feet and helped her along her way. She was injured, but she could make it. He helped her limp along. Soon she could walk on her own.

He then saw a little boy along the path. He was discouraged and starting to cry. He looked up as the man came by. He lifted his hat with a little bit of hope in his eyes. The man was about to offer encouraging words when the pelting began again, but this time a little harder. They started with the bigger rocks and then went to arrows filled with flame. The whole shaft of the arrow was on fire as they must have soaked it in some sort of gasoline or fuel.

But, once again, he was able to turn his shield toward the attack and pray it away.

He knew the attacks were coming again, so he worked quickly. He wanted the boy to go home, so he took him on his back and gave him a piggyback ride most of the way across the field until he was close to the other side, where the boy said he lived. He dropped off the boy safely on the other side. And the boy ran off into the forest and turned back with a slight wave and disappeared into the forest.

As he turned around, he noticed the enemy forces had grown.

Now he had to get back. The enemy had followed him. They had pelted him and now they were in full force.

He realized he couldn't do this alone, so he knelt.

He was on one knee, almost as helpless as he could get, and the enemy was surrounding him and closing in. He muttered a few words under his breath and as the enemy grew closer, he didn't move. As a matter of fact, instead of getting up to fight, he knelt even farther toward the ground. He was almost lying flat, and his lips were still moving. The enemy couldn't hear what he was saying as his words were silent, but they could see the fervency from his face.

He prayed.

His enemy army was almost defeated even before they began to fight … for he knew a truth and then it started.

There was a rumbling in the trees behind the enemy. The clouds had started to form. The tree tops started to sway toward them and back. He stopped.

"Father."

And a burst of air came toppling the trees, and there was an army twice the size of the existing enemy army who came to his rescue. They started to fight and bloodshed filled the air. The turmoil was palpable. It was unending, so it seemed—and the whoosh of flame and fire and smoke went up into the air, and they were all gone.

He fell to his knees again and said, "Thank you, Father." And he fell asleep.

He woke up, and he was still in his cabin. He must have fallen asleep before going outside. But then he heard it again. A pelting on his door.

15. COAL – " LIGHT ON THE OUTSIDE "

It was as cold and hard as a stone.

Its light could not be seen.

It was in a deep, dark place in the bottom of the earth.

But now it is aflame.

It is burning bright for all to see.

This, which was once a hard piece of coal, is now here to resonate His love.

16. ADAPTING – "TO THE WILL OF GOD"

There is a way things work. And try as you might, they will not work differently. There is a spiritual realm, and you do not control the spiritual realm. God is in charge. No matter how much you might like to be or I might like to be, we are not in charge. There are other forces at work here.

Look at a battery.

Sitting on its own, it can do nothing. It needs to be plugged in the proper place. I have a remote for my TV, and I can click all I want but if it doesn't have batteries, it won't turn on. It is made to work a certain way with the batteries.

You cannot do it alone. You need God's Holy Spirit to work in you. You need the battery.

But I also look at an adapter. I have a cell phone that I could plug into the wall. I could push the plug into the socket repeatedly, and it will not make it in because it was not meant to go there. I need an adapter; I need to go with it the way it was meant to work. I want to work with it according to its rules, because that's the way it was meant to work. But now I have an adapter, and it works great. It fits perfectly, and the energy flows the way it was meant to.

Wall plug.

A switch on a wall is the same way. You can switch it up and down, but what if it is the push-in kind of switch? It won't switch if you try to push it up and down. It won't work. It will only work in the way it was meant to.

We have two switches by our front door: one for the light inside, and one for the light outside over the steps. We can try to push that up and down, but it was meant to go left and right.

There is a way we could try to force something to work, or in humility we can work it the way it was meant to work—and it will work much better.

Now look at a clock.

A clock is a representation of time. It is not time itself. So if you switch a clock forward an hour or behind, you are not changing time; you are only changing how we perceive time. It is a physical representation of a spiritual truth.

The physical things we see in our physical world cannot change the reality of the spiritual realm. Even though we can change them, it doesn't change what's happening spiritually.

We have the church, a physical building, or the Bible, a physical book. But a physical building can only represent the body of Christ in a physical way. The spiritual realm is other.

A physical book—the Bible—can only represent in words—flat on a page—what is happening around us in the spiritual realm. The wall is not the socket. The socket is not the light. The light is not the electricity. But they all work together, needing each other to represent the truth.

We live in a spiritual realm, but we can't always see it. We only have physical representations of what is happening in the spiritual realm.

17. RICE – " SATURATE OUR SOUL "

I have a big pot of soup. It is stirring my soul, warm on a cold day.

It is saturated with water—with broth—and it puffs up big. It is saturated in my soul.

My beauty is gone but bestowed again. My life is gone, but brought back again with food.

I am saturated. It is a mystery.

I was hard, and white and crispy, but now I am full and flowing over from the soul.

18. JACK THE GIANT – " HUMILITY "

Once upon a time, there was a boy named Jack. He was 10 feet tall. Not too ordinary for a boy. He was 10 feet tall, and everybody knew about it. His mother knew and his father knew and his friends knew and everybody in his town knew. He was proud of it and let everybody know.

He knew how to swing a bat and box a cat. He knew how to find a friend by jumping over a fence. He was not very good at hide and seek, as all his friends could see him.

He loved to jump in the garden and make things grow. He loved to plant tall plants and pick the fruits off of the top where no one else could reach.

He loved to play in the grass and play hopscotch in one leap and a bound. He was 10 feet tall, and everybody knew it.

He wasn't a mean boy, but he was very aware of his height.

He sought it out—opportunities to use it.

He would jump up to bridges and down lanes and all his friends could exclaim how fast he was.

But one day ... he saw a giant.

Now this wasn't any ordinary giant. This giant was 5,000 feet tall. He was so tall that you could hardly see his head in the clouds. He had delicate wisps of clouds around his forehead that he would look up at and blow away with a mighty gust from his mouth. And he would whirl the clouds with his hand and make them stream away from him in a wind across the sky.

Everybody was amazed at this new giant. But not Jack.

He wanted to be the proud new thing that everybody was talking about. He wanted to be the tallest and the fastest and the strongest—and for everyone to look up to him. But not now.

This new giant was in the way, casting a shadow on his cause. Making him look like he wasn't as much as he was. But he was. And he knew it. He knew he was still the fastest and the best, and he would let everyone know it.

He looked up at the giant and said, "You … up … there."

The giant looked down from the sky with a smile on his face and said, "Hello down there."

Now Jack didn't like this, because he wasn't to be looked down upon. But the moment when Jack was about to yell again, the giant reached down from his mighty place and put Jack on his hand and lifted him.

He was going past mountains and trees. The birds flying by were getting smaller beneath him when suddenly, the giant let him down on a big ledge on the top of a large mountain.

He stopped. He stared. He could see the giant eye to eye. And he said, "Hey mister, what are you doing putting me way up here?"

The giant got close to Jack and said, "I have something for you. I have a plentiful garden, and I want to show you."

Jack looked puzzled. "What do you mean a garden? Way up here? In the clouds and the sun
and the rocky top of the mountain?"

"Go and see," said the giant.

Jack got off the ledge. He hopped over a few rocks and came down on the other side of a little hill. And after he got down off the hill, he started to walk over the finest ground he had ever seen. He had seen hills like this before, but nothing that rich. The soil was black with moisture, with not a stone in sight.

He reached down and sifted it through his fingers. Pressing it between his thumb and forefingers. He thought it was soft and moist and sweet like he had never seen before.

The giant looked at him and nodded his head in a knowing way. "Pretty nice, eh?"

"Yeah," said Jack. "And where did you get this?"

"It's been here all along," replied the giant.

Jack continued to sift the soil through his fingers and said to the giant, "Can I work it? Can I make the soil push up some big old plants? Can I make them grow?"

"Yes, of course," said the giant. "You can work it as long as you like."

So he started to work the soil but he noticed the more he worked it, the coarser it got. He would take a hoe and dig into the ground and rocks would appear underneath where he had made his mark.

He wanted to be better, so he tried harder. He would make long, smooth strokes and that didn't work. He hacked at the soil, digging deeper into it—

and that still didn't work. Larger rocks seemed to appear the more he forced into it.

But then something happened. The giant spoke. "Walk away."

But there was no way he would walk away from this. He knew there was something to it that he could do, so he tried harder. But the more he hit the soil, the more the rocks grew.

He begged the giant: "Why is this soil so hard? Why don't you do something?"

But when the giant again suggested he walk away, he wouldn't have any part of it. So he persisted. And he persisted. And he persisted. Until finally he fell down in exhaustion. He couldn't do it.

The giant said, "Walk away."

So he did.

He got on his feet, brushed off his knees and hands and started to walk slowly ... in defeat to the edge of the garden.

He sat down—disappointed—in the grass. He couldn't believe his eyes. As he sat there, patiently, the rocks started to grow. And they led to one another in a little pathway. They formed a loop around the garden and shunned all from the outside. And the garden started to grow. It grew and it grew and it grew until it was 90-feet tall. It was filled with plants of orange and green and beautiful pink with flowers on them. And they smelled so sweet. And there were melons and grapefruit, vegetables and fruits from every season growing all in one special place. It was plentiful.

There was more food than he could eat in a lifetime, and it kept growing, kept reproducing. As long as he would take one fruit off the tree, another would grow in its place of a different color. There was an endless array.
A variety.

When he was over the shock and the confusion of what had just happened, he came to his senses and remembered the giant standing behind him.

He looked back over his shoulder to see what the giant was up to, because he had heard a sound.

His shoulders were shaking—the giant's. And his lips were moving and a big grin had spread across his face. He let out a big roar of laughter. He was so excited that he could hardly contain himself. And he stomped his foot in joy, and he loved every moment of what had just happened.

He loved it.

He loved to see the joy on Jack's face. The excitement, the wonder, the mystery all in one expression. The giant just laughed—overwhelmed with an outrageous joy. His story had been seen. It had played out in Jack's life, and he had someone to share it with. He was excited by the very reason that Jack had missed.

He had been missing the point all along … for above his head a cloud had appeared. It had spread out over the ground. When Jack thought back to his first glance at the giant, he remembered his lips moving. And what he was saying was indiscreet. An immense cloud had formed out of the mouth of the giant, and the mist rose over the garden and it came down as an invisible rain to replenish the garden.

You see, the reason the giant had wanted Jack to move was so that he could allow the rain to come down. He couldn't do that while Jack was in the way. He had to move. He had to make his peace and move into the giant's guidance, because the giant had done all this before.

And he knew what he was doing.

19. BARBEQUE – " PEACE "

Peace is like a thick sauce that you brush all over a rack of ribs.

20. CATAPULT TOY – " PERCEPTION "

We went out east this summer, and my son got a copper Catapult Toy.

We were near the Mayflower in a little shop where my son and his cousin were playing with the toy. My brother—his uncle—got it for my son, and he brought it home. It now sits on our little shelf in the kitchen.

It is a burnished copper. Brownish in most parts but scraped off and worn to make it look old. There is a lever on its side that works. My son and his cousin put tiny stones in it and watched them fly off as they played.

But this is a perception of the reality. We won't go back to ancient England, and put large boulders into heavy hand-crafted stocks of wood bolted together by large spikes and hammered with a heavy anvil that a man, except a very muscular man, could hardly lift.

We won't stand at the bottom of it and look up 30 feet into the sun to see the top of the wooden arches and beams reaching into the sun, or being drenched with dew on a rainy or foggy day.

But we will see a little toy and imagine it so.

It is all a perception of the reality of what actually happened. We can see it in our mind's eye as if it happened. Because it did.

There were army soldiers and captains. People yelling commands to "Hit the deck" or "Run," as boulders came flying at them.

There is a reality. And … a perceived reality.

Sometimes we don't even think of the reality when we see that little toy. We just see a toy on a shelf that gets bumped off sometimes, as we go on about our day with this pencil sharpener of a toy.

21. THE TIME MACHINE – " CONTROL "

I once went to a man's house who had a time machine. This wasn't the type of time machine you would think of on the Sci-Fi channel, which brings you back in time to the age of the dinosaurs or Columbus or Britain at various times in history. This was a different type of time machine that controlled his own time. In his own way. It was mostly for himself. And hardly anyone else knew about it.

His name was Fred.

He was 16 years old when the adventure began. He had moved into a new house in Maine. He was living by the shore, near Bangor, Maine down by the rocks and the trees and the old roads. His grandparents had lived there before them in the 1980s but had long since passed away.

When they moved there, the first thing he noticed was the large gravel trucks whizzing by at 7:00 a.m. The trucks were going nowhere fast.

He woke up one morning early to the sound of the trucks. The sun was shining against the white cloth curtains in his window, so he opened the window and the shade to enjoy the morning air.

He decided to get up early and explore the house.

He walked outside and saw the bulkhead. For those of you not familiar with new England homes, a bulkhead is a slanted door on the side of the house that most often, when opened, had cement steps inside it leading down to the basement.

Now this was an older home—probably over 100 years old. The basement was full of dirt and cement blocks. It wasn't what you would call clean. It was mostly to hold up the house and not for major recreation or entertaining. One would hardly go down there except to store things or to check the furnace or change a light.

The other way down to the basement was down the stairs from the inside of the house. They would creek and were made from old 2 x 8 boards that his grandfather must have replaced along the way.

But the basement was clean, except for the occasional spider web along the rafters.

As Fred looked in, coming down the cement stairs from the outside, the light shone on the floor but not much farther.

He reached around the corner to find the light switch and turned it on. The light bulbs hung from the ceiling from between the wooden rafters, and had a pull string as to turn them off and on.

As he walked through the dimly lit basement, he could see a pile of sand in one corner. He went around another corner, past the furnace into almost what was like a hallway area.

He looked into the far distant corner into what was another sand pile against what appeared to be stones cemented together as another part of the foundation.

There was a little area that he had to dig away in the sand to see what was back there. As his eyes had started to adjust from the outside light, he noticed a little glimmer of something in the back corner, mostly covered with sand.

He knew it wasn't glass, as the glimmer wasn't sharp enough. It was kind of a dull glimmer. It must have been metal of some sort.

So he dug away at the sand to make space for his body to slide through over the mound of dirt.

He came onto the other side and had to wipe cobwebs from his face. It appeared to him as a bar of metal cut into the dirt, so he made his way over to this metal contraption to try to figure out the rest of it and what it was.

When he got there, he could see the bar of metal more clearly, and his eyes had further adjusted to the light. He would have to bring a flashlight down the next time he came. But his curiosity got the best of him. He started to dig around the edges of this metal bar, which he now realized had been rusted from years of this moist air. And as he dug down farther, he came across a handle made of wood.

It looked like a large metal screw on the inside, about six inches long, which only showed on the top with the rest of the wooden handle around it.

It had writing on the edge that he could hardly decipher, but only came to realize with a smile that it was "Made in Taiwan."

No mystery there. Yet.

As he uncovered more of the contraption, he discovered the metal tubing was welded together at various angles with different types of handles on each part.

Some had levers. Some moved. Some didn't.

Some moved the whole bar, others had chains that connected two of the bars together. It was difficult to make sense of what it all was, but it was intriguing.

He was finally able to pull the whole contraption up from the sand. He pulled it on to the concrete floor and dusted off the sand.

He could see it was old and fragile. Missing pieces as far as he could tell.

He leaned it up against the wall, as it was heavy.

He tried to pull one of the levers but to no avail. He went out to the bulkhead and into the old three-car garage and found some oil to put into the old joints. He got back just in time to see a slight movement on its own.

It must have been settling into its new position, leaned up against the wall. He squirted the oil into the various joints and levers to allow them to move more freely. There were also gears and turn styles that needed a little adjusting. With enough squirts of oil and a little pressure, they started to adjust.

First the wooden handle and then the old metal gear. And as he cranked them both together at the same time, a shimmer went through the air. It was almost like a wave or a ripple with the air around him condensing into a ripple-like shape. He couldn't see parts of the furnace and the wall for a little while, and then they came back into focus.

He walked back upstairs a little confused. As he entered the kitchen, he noticed that it was 7:00 a.m. And he was sure that was the time he had gotten up that morning, but dismissed it as misreading the clock as he passed by it earlier.

The next day his curiosity got the best of him, and he went down to the contraption again.

He lifted it up and shifted a few more levers.

This time when he went upstairs, the curtains had changed color and the lights had changed colors as well.

The funny thing is that this was something he had been planning to do, but just hadn't gotten to it yet. Apparently sometime in the process of moving the levers, these things had been done in the right timing.

He couldn't quite figure out how these things were happening, but he certainly didn't mind—as they worked out just as he had planned.

But then something happened. Instead of him just wondering how this happened, he almost started to expect that it would happen.

He would switch a lever here or pull a handle there and twist a gear in different combinations, and things would happen. He would search all around the house to see what happened next.

He liked to be able to control it all from one spot. No more worries, things just started to get done until next time. And he spent more time doing it, too. He waited on it, could hardly wait to get down there and make the changes. And his house was really coming together.

Next thing he knew, his chores were done all around the house.

But he wanted more. He kept fixating on it from night to day, expecting something to happen, trying to control something else. But nothing happened.

Then he tried to put on the straps that had been hanging off this thing and just getting in the way the whole time. He strapped them around his wrists and his forearms. It was almost as if he was one with the machine.

He would move one way and several of the arms moved in simultaneous motion. He would shift; they would make a parallel motion. He would move one of his limbs—the bar closes his arm or leg, whichever he was lifting would lift as well in complete parallel union. He was becoming one with the machine. Inseparable.

But then he noticed the machine would start to move. And as it moved, he moved in complete parallel motion. What was once under his control was no longer his to control. He got angry. He got scared. He tried to push harder, but to no avail.

This had gotten him now into its trap. He had not tried to, but the more he did—the more he tried to get out—the more he was trapped. Like struggling in quicksand. One false move makes another and another even more desperate move.

It was controlling him.

Then he heard a voice.

From upstairs—outside the basement on the lawn.

The realtor had stopped by to see how they were settling into their new house. He was talking to Fred's parents and as he was about to leave, he heard Fred's faint voice from the basement.

He stepped down each cement step carefully and peered into the basement and saw Fred's forsaken face. He was scared but relieved to see somebody.

"I see you found it," said the realtor. "The previous owners left it here and tried to hide it as they hadn't wanted to take it with them, but were hoping no one would find it and get into the havoc it causes.

"I have a key they gave me just in case something like this happened. But it's out of your reach. As a matter of fact, even if it was within your reach, you wouldn't be able to use it. I tried it once myself. You see, there is something about having someone else do it that loosens the connections. Maybe because it's not the same person. A separate, unattached force. But whatever the reason, it seems to work."

So the realtor reached up and into the shadows behind one of the wooden beams on the ceiling. He felt around and found an old nail with the key on a wire ring hanging from it.

He pulled it down and jammed it hard into a keyhole he had found on the end of one of the bars. Fred never would have been able to find it on his own. From where he was strapped in, it wasn't even visible. It was out of reach.

Then the realtor said something important.

"OK, on the count of three, while I am still holding the key, I am going to push it extra hard into the keyhole and at the same time you need to let go of all the controls, and you will be free."

"Ready," he exclaimed. "One, two, three."

And he was free.

22. BEHAVIOR – " WALKING IN THE SPIRIT "

The sky was blurry as his eyes readjusted to the light. He had been laying in the middle of the forest and had just woken up. He must have been knocked out. The back of his head was hurting.

He didn't remember a lot at the moment and couldn't remember quite where he was.

He got up and brushed the pine needles off his back as best he could and brushed down the back of his legs and arms.

He sat up and remembered a group of guys he had been with.

Where had they gone?

There was a leader of the group who was big and stocky. His arms were the size of the boy's two legs put together.

He was starting to become more aware now. There were 14 of them running rampant in the forest, taking whatever they wanted and living their own lives. For themselves.

He had become a part of them several months before when he had gotten lost in the back woods of his father's castle. He had wandered too far from home. He had been walking down the long stretch of lawn and then through the back gate. He crossed a mighty river over rocks and sticks and quite a strong current. At this point, it had gotten dark and when he tried to turn back, he had gotten turned around.

He had met these other boys when he was wandering around in the dark. They had flashlights.
He followed them home to their cave, but wouldn't have any part of what they were doing at first.

But when it started to get fun and reckless, he started to enjoy it as many a boy would. Having friends doing heroic things. Picking on others. Starting to feel strong.

But as the months went on, he started to miss his home.

He then realized he had especially missed his father. He dearly loved his mother and little sister as well, but he was at a growing age where he was now trying to be a man.

And the trying is what had gotten him into trouble.

But now after several months with these boys, he was trying to get home.

He thought it was good to try on his own. But it's also nice not to do it alone. The more he tried on his own, the more lost he got. He could tell a little bit from the stars at night the general direction, but that was about it. He couldn't go very far at night, so his main option was to try to get back during the day and everything looked the same. From the bushes to the trees to the fields. In whatever direction he tried to go, it seemed like he was going the wrong direction.

And to make matters worse, the others in the group didn't want him to go.

He had been taking part in their little scams and mischievous ways and hadn't realized how far he had gotten. But they knew if he could escape, he would go his own way and maybe tell someone the things he had done and get them into trouble.

So they wouldn't let him go.

So when he woke up with a bump on his head, he realized it was because he had tried to make his way home and these boys thought the worst of it.

But they were nowhere around, so this was his chance.

He reached in his pocket and found a medallion he had long forgotten. He hadn't had much use for it at the time, so he had all but forgotten it. It was a medallion that his father had given him. He didn't know why or what use it would be, but he loved it.

It had engraved in it—like a compass—a star pointing north, south, east and west.

He held the cold metal in his hands and as he pressed it harder and thought of home, it started to glow.

He had never noticed that before. He had had it for a long time and maybe it was related to the fact that he had never wished for home. Once he did, it started to light up in the general direction he thought of his home.

He was astonished.

Why hadn't he ever seen this before?

He guessed it was because he had never wanted to.

He put it around his neck with the leather strap that was through a hole in the medallion.

He strapped it on tight so that he wouldn't lose it, and he started to walk in the general direction of the arrow on the compass that was lit up.

If he would step out of line, the next arrow in the circle would light up, leading him back to the original direction. He wanted to go home, and this was leading him.

When he let go of the medallion, it would stop as if he didn't need it anymore. But every time he put his focus on it and walked forward and put it close to his chest, it would light up again.

His heart was an especially efficient tool for lighting up. It was almost as if it could sense the heart's presence. He didn't know if it was the pumping of the heart; but whatever it was when it was near his heart, there was far more clarity and purpose in the medallion's leading.

He soon reached the river he had crossed. He remembered the certain sticks and the rocks jutting out of the river. He was on his way home for sure now. When he tried to remember all the ways to go, he got a little fuzzy; but even if he would get way off the path without holding onto the medallion, as soon as he would look back at it and allow it to do its thing, he was corrected in his path.

A willingness and a purpose. That was all he needed.

23. MIKE & LINDA – "RELATIONSHIP WITH GOD"

Once upon a time there was a great romance. Mike loved Linda, and Linda loved Mike. They lived in the same house together; they raised children together; they loved each other. Until one day it happened.

Mike went out of the house and forgot about Linda. He walked around. Foraged in trash. Went around the neighborhood looking for who knows what. He was lost. He couldn't find her, and he didn't know he was looking for her.

One day he found a note in his pocket! It was a grocery list. He went to the store, forgetting why he was going and bought the groceries for Linda unbeknownst to him.

Now he had a bag full of groceries, and he didn't know why. He had a bag full of groceries he didn't know what to do with, so he started giving them away to random people.

One day he ran into Linda. She asked what he was doing. He said he had found a random list in his pocket and was giving away the groceries.

"Do you know why you are giving the groceries away?" asked Linda.

"No," he replied.

"Because I gave you the list," she said. "It was to do together. For us to share. Now we can go about doing what we were meant to do. Being together and sharing with others."

24. THE PRAYERS BELOW THE SURFACE –"DIRT"

At the edge of the woods, there is a quiet place to enter. Enter still. As the raging wind outside the woods come and go, few enter.

There is a doubt in their mind that it will be a quiet place—that will be still—but it is.

Made in the USA
Lexington, KY
21 August 2017